# Every Living Day

# Praise for Adam Gianforcaro

"absolutely striking, full of heart, and a detailed approach to the science of the human condition—Gianforcaro's words reflect the light of being alive, being in the here and now. the poems trumpet an iridescent queerness; sing the significance of joy; traverse the universe of the body and the body of the universe. *Every Living Day* is an achievement of the unlimited beauty of our every day."

—luna rey hall, author of *loudest when startled* and *space neon neon space*

"Adam Gianforcaro's *Every Living Day* bears testimony to a world certain of its destruction. As conductor of this swelling symphony of a collection, Gianforcaro declares, "I have always had a thing for curtains parting," and guides us through searing existential concerns wrought with explorations of terror, complicity, grief, culpability, and power. With striking musicality and metaphors that weave the gamut of (im)possibility, each poem dons its life on the stage after the parted curtains and barrels towards their closing, only to meet air and fire—but then: a whisper, movement, a light through uncharted darkness, a promise that there is, despite all odds, an after. *Every Living Day* will wrench your veins with heartache and hope, and you will be better for it. I could not recommend this collection and this poet more highly; this book is a must-have for your shelves."

—Mandy Moe Pwint Tu, author of *Monsoon Daughter* and *Unsprung*

"Adam Gianforcaro's *Every Living Day* is a love letter to the vastness of spacetime, from the pinholes to nebulas, and all of the experience of existence in between. He is both astrophysicist and philosopher as he explores mycelium and the multiverse, sung in hymnals to the sun, sauna, & self. This is as much a poetry collection as a book of hymns, anthologizing corporeal experience and unpacking anxiety & depression. Gianforcaro asks simultaneously, What are we apart from? and What are we a part of? What's in the aftermath, and is there pre-existence? The (queer) self as steam, vapor, something that sticks deeper– you will feel this collection in your head, heart, and bones."

—Alison Lubar, author of *Philosophers Know Nothing About Love* and *queer feast*


"Adam Gianforcaro has written the book that I wish I could give a younger version of myself, a collection of deep understanding, suffering and unfathomable freedom from it. Gianforcaro interrogates trauma, the devastating things that are "so mundane until it's married to someone you love" and frees itself inside its own verse. This is a collection that has done the hard work of understanding itself, and when these poems aren't yearning, they are celebrating a full, chosen life, a life that begs "for what is existence if not vigor?"

—Gardner Dorton, author of *Stone Fruit*

"Theory: it starts and ends with fire. In this collection of poetry that is as honeyed as it is honed, Adam Gianforcaro returns us to such simple, burning truths—both cosmically humid and deeply human alike. *Every Living Day* is an invitation to warm yourself, whether by sauna steam or ballooning sun; it is a door left open, a gentle portal to all that is possible; it is "A greeting, a pull, / a tenacious tugging…" Theory: somewhere in spacetime you are already reading these poems—and oh, how very lucky you are."

—Ashley Cline, author of & *watch how easily the jaw sings of god*

# Every Living Day

Poems

Adam Gianforcaro

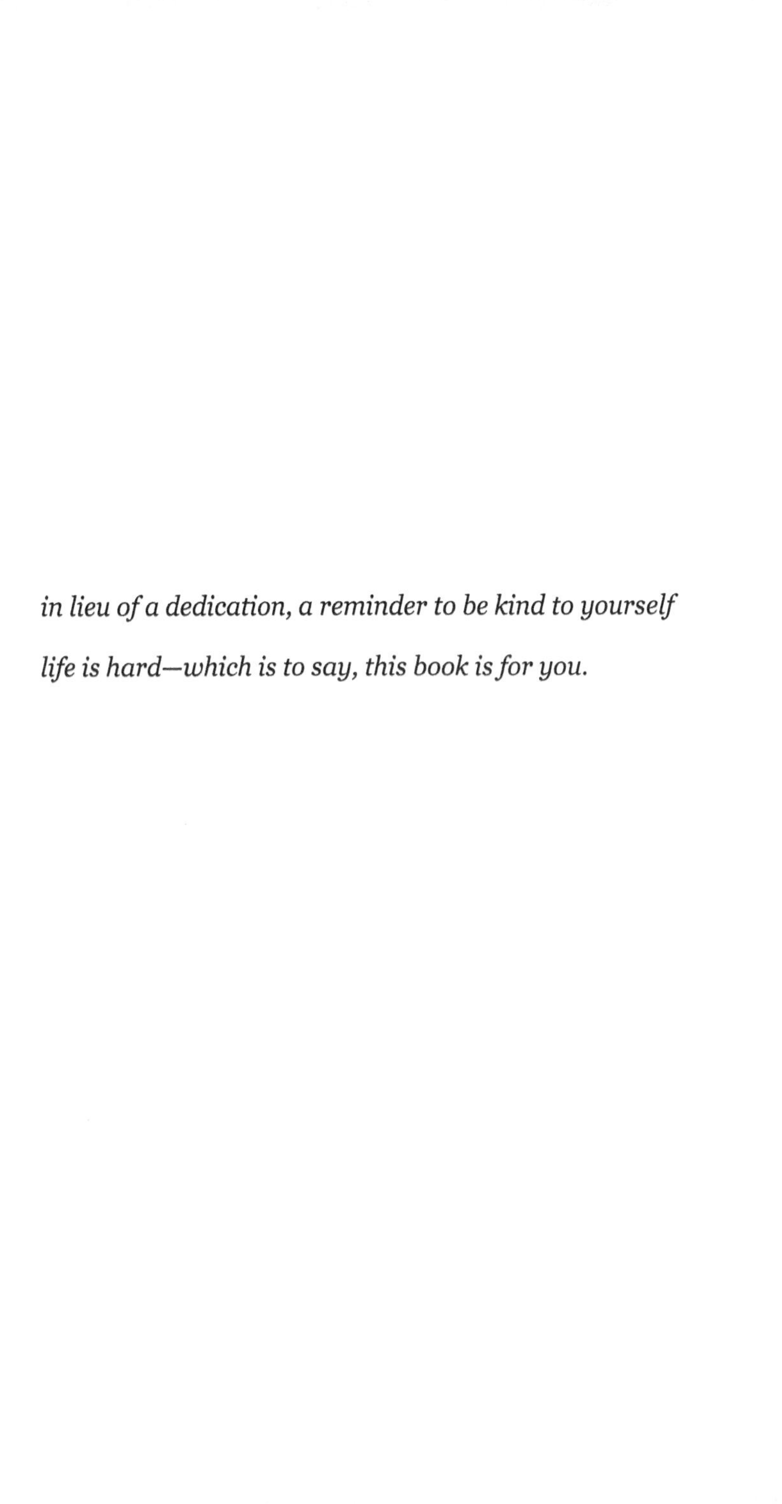

*in lieu of a dedication, a reminder to be kind to yourself*

*life is hard—which is to say, this book is for you.*

*As revenge for my burning*
*I burned the whole world*
*And was warm for a little while*

—Mount Eerie

# Table of Contents

I.

# Overture

The way in which sound
comes and goes and echoes

so feverishly. The world
inside and outside

like two shoulders
that never knew they were shoulders

despite the weight
placed on top of them.

Don't forget about the open window
and how it whispers breathily.

And what is a window
but a lover, a fable? Day

in her daylight gown,
the sun singing folk songs again,

singing skies
in the key of *Wheat Field*

*with Cypresses*. If anything,
don't forget about the window

who was kind enough earlier
to mention the doorway

in its reflection.

## Every Living Day

To give up convenience, to wear patience like walls
draped in soot. To do no harm.

I try my best. But the little I do seems so little.

Map out the landfills. Bury yourself in plastic.
Every novelty cup filled to the brim
with unbearable, living pain.
O Sorrowful Earth, this is sorrow overflowing.
The streets are flooded with it.
Fish swim right up to our doorsteps.
The scary kind, too, with headlamps
and daggers for teeth.

When I can no longer kneel, I will wade myself
toward repentance, beg forgiveness—
for folding banana peels in tin foil,
for drinking coffee from a Keurig.

Every living day I fuck the earth with negligence.

Earlier this summer, I ran over a mouse
with the lawnmower. Sliced it in half
like the ocean divorcing the sky.
And the mouse was a newborn, with mama mouse
giving birth to her second pup right there
in that verdant patch of trauma.

As if to live without harm is to be born into the blade.

And as it happened, while the mouse
twitched itself into stillness,
I thought immediately of this silly song
from summer camp: *It's cheese, cheese,*
*cheese that makes the mice go 'round.*
We'd squeak our campfire voices
and wave our arms like ribbons.

The last verse of the song goes like this,
and we would scream it as loud as we could:
*IT'S LOVE, LOVE,*
*LOVE THAT MAKES THE WORLD GO 'ROUND!*

What is love if not sharp and spinning
and smelling of earth?

The truth is harder to swallow. And the truth is this:
I am a terrible partner.
I tell the Earth I'm sorry, write halfhearted elegies
for field mice, only to fall victim
to fast fashion and Amazon Prime.

What I mean is this: I try my best
when it is convenient to do so.

And now I'll zoom out, place the blame elsewhere,
create alternate histories
to make myself seem less culpable.
Privilege is the planet from which all of this is possible.
Convenience is a world on fire.

And to give up that convenience, to do no harm.
I'll pretend to not know the answer when I ask, *But how*?

## As If Pleading

This is the part where the trumpet comes in:
hollow, heartsick horn. Scene that follows the flowers

in reverse, which would be precisely the same scene
if shown in the forward motion time seems to favor.
Always a hungry earth.

We could all be flowers on film, considering
that's precisely what we are. We reach toward the sun

as if pleading, which, of course, is precisely why we do it.
And this ground from which we pull ourselves,
this game of lie-in-wait:

it's our way of playing lived-in, as if waking every day
meant more than waiting for the earth's
mud-caked lips to part.

Life is a lifetime of waiting in an otherwise finite world.
Fierce yawn playing game-of-wind.
And it's in this way the film continues,

capturing movement while it can
in its ever so pleading way,

as if to say, *When you're ready, my dear,*
*the ground will hug you*
*back into the land—*

# Dog Days

Spit into the mouth of the season
and wish it a good morning. Phlegm

like clover and clouds
named for the names shared with us

by the breeze: sweet pea, rose,
Julianne-dabbed-with-Burberry-eau—

and O the way the blues and greens
refuse to clash in this wardrobe of a walking path.

Give the day the leftover dust of sidewalk chalk
and it will hopscotch its way into afternoon.

Lunch is lemonade and bee stings, with apple butter
and whatever the end piece of the bread is called.

Above us, a cloud we christened Propagate
splits in two then disappears altogether.

You flick fire ants from your ankle and pretend
there isn't a prophecy in their tiny hot tickles.

Look around. When light is blocked, we can still see
inside the sycamore's shadow. Now what was it

you said about prophecy? Never mind—
we're leaving now. The car is hot

then cold then hot again. At home, there is no
swimming pool but we pretend. We float on the lawn

and dive face first into the dried-up garden.
When we come-to, the moon's holding hands

with the sun again. But soon, the moon will loosen
its grip. Soon, the sun will free fall from the bluff.

On the ground, tradition has insects picking pieces
of our suitor's gore, bringing bits of sparkle

back to life—until later, all the day's light
and all the day's shine will suffocate

in the glass jars of children who know better.
And behind their bedroom windows:

one large and looming shadow.

# Renewal

We wake in a clearing
and walk, shimmy
between cornhusks
to a field of falling afternoon
where we are greeted
with fire, with far-off stream sounds
and later, when a sharp chill
cloaks the flames, we lie
like two instruments,
two contiguous states
curled together, closer
than winter's homecoming—
our bodies a half-heated sauna
rising like steam,
kicking our weightless legs
through solstice skies
and landing somewhere soft,
somewhere new, which looks more
or less like another clearing
until, again, the fire.

## Soon

Soon: the sport
of spinach leaves,

an earthly game
of too-much becomes too-little.

~

A single sliver of light
like one side

of the double-slit experiment,
yet in its coiling

almost Fibonaccian.
Fetal in a way

and terrifying too:
the way in which one retreads,

the way a body
becomes darkness.

~

And the way a body,
curved and cratered,

becomes magnetic,
a geophysical blip,

then nothing—

# Poolside with a Paperback

DeLillo begins chapter five this way, says: *Let's enjoy
these aimless days while we can.* I think, Yes, precisely.
A page later, a character confesses this, says: *I want
to immerse myself in American magic and dread.*
I think, Yes, yes, that's it. Such are summers and pop songs.
The way everything is distraction. Soon, a chemical cloud
will enter the novel. I think, Yes, of course. And I consider
the sun, count the willful ways it harms and heals.
Like a kind of lover, an entire government.
I want to read more but it's hard to concentrate:
the music, the muggy air, the horrible way
sunscreen makes my skin feel. The frenzy
of public pools, how everything shines so unpleasantly.
Sweat beads lotion-white on my chest, the slick
of the paperback even slicker with oily fingers.
I look up from the book and into a looming black.
I think chemical warfare. I think magic.

# Nine Panels

[1]

Queer is the portal through which
we find ourselves. Poem with pipe
fittings. Pipe dream. Pushed
through drains and out again.
The taste of copper, the slick
of PVC. Porcelain cold like mornings.
And all day long, the man in shadows.
There is wind, a calling for. The man
pushing forward as to not fall backward
from the in-frame dark. A sink
full of body hair. A piece of it on your tongue.

[2]

Inside is outside no matter how many walls
we stand up. The living we do, the dividing
and hiding of dirt. The hinges of existence.

Underfoot is a world so small it stirs up infinity.
Pieces of our shedding selves. Symbols everywhere.
Kafka's *Metamorphosis* no matter which moments

come to mind. We count forward and backward,
by breaks and fractions. The decimal point
nothing more than a cluster of dust.

[3]

The rule of thirds has us here now,
            everything precisely in place,
      staring at our feet as if to accept
where we stand. And now a voice.
            Says, *I need this piece of you to stay
      here*. And I comply. My reflection now

                                          across the hall

somewhere.

[4]

A few excerpts from [REDACTED]:

*—a cellar door—*
*—just then the clock—*
*—boy in total darkness—*
*—the King—*
*—the King is overjoyed—*
*—he cried—*
*—he cried—*
*—he cried—*
*—he—*

[5]

Boy in darkness. Total.

The dark surrounding the surrounding dark.

Prelude in E minor caught in echoes.

[6]

O blessed light,
          we're not far now.
O luminous mouth,
          keep pulling us in.
Shadow of the under-
          pass, boy from the book.
O luminous mouth,
          O portal, today
I dipped my toe
          into the event horizon.

[7]

Forward and backward. Symbols everywhere.
A dividing underfoot.

O blessed light, remove us from the frame.
Take us from the dark.

Take us. Take us.

[8]

We make our way back
to porcelain. Self-concept
as sink drain. Mushroom cap
with a hobby for collecting things.
Says, *I need this piece of you.*
But which piece? For how long?
Self-portrait as missing faucet.
Still-life with life at a standstill.
But then time passes. And time
is king, isn't it?

[9]

Queer is a portal. Sink of body hair.
No kings. Only the event horizon.
It stirs up infinity. It takes us.

# Queer Love Story

Bless us hellions with love
but not enough. I'm afraid

that story's been told. Survival
was our first matrimony.

You look to us with two eyes
as two fists clenched

between the burning sun
and your burning sons—

O! Now here comes the choir,
discreet everymen with harps

and horns and yearnings, closing in
around our figures in flames:

prophets picnicking with gasoline.
Still, dogma dangles us from the balcony

like the King of Pop. Queer kids
spell trauma for every camera

they see. Anchors ask, What is it like
to kiss with the forked tongue of a sinner?

Like heaven, we say. Like a burning.

## Not Everyone Thinks of the Festival When Hearing About Burning Man

Because our stories
are rooted in fire.

Lattice limbs and torsos
slick with spit and kerosene.

Homos, heretics: human
bodies as woodpile,

as Sunday matinee.
Twigs piled and pressed

like lovers in heat.
But I am afraid of fire

so I dress it in drag. A retelling
in radiance: rope-tied bodies

as stained-glass sculptures,
flames as stage lights.

Let the glow pierce our skin
but gently. Let us

no longer fear our neighbors.

# Fever Dream as Cardio

First, I am dream with gym shorts
under sweatpants. Then I am dream
with crowbar. That is, I wake

in the locker room to the sound of faggot
on a straight man's tongue. I dream
of turning the tides, dream it into being.

Is it just me or does the word *pry*
sound incomplete? And yet body parts leak
and swell. Think of this leaking, this swelling,

as anything but phallic. Think brains instead.
Think the sound of a can opening, the smell
of ground meat in a gym bag. I keep going.

Act two has me heading for the elliptical. I see
the man with tongue behind me in wall mirrors.
My pores pump shrapnel. My skin itches. Somewhere

behind me: a monologue, a discovery.
I consider logistics. A nontarget's privilege.
The prophecies of passing. When I dream

I am always dream with crowbar, a lust
for bones experimenting with role play.
I have always had a thing for curtains parting.

# In Which the Sauna Becomes a Sacrament

Light through lattice
like a basket holding
the sun: wound-weaver,

unburdener. We walk
in and out of heat
like homes, in and out

of thoughts like sweat
seeping from skin
and drying there.

What happens?
Do we pull ourselves
in again, suck back

our salt and water-selves?
Such strange bodies:
stretching, shriveling,

soaking wet. The shadows
we cast. Walls we put up—
clay and charcoal, worlds

of forest and stone.
This is the flesh of being
and what remains: skin cells

asking to stay put
when our deeper selves
plead so pitifully otherwise.

# Condensation

body after body
                    streaming
      from shower-
heads
      the rush of river
rush of bodies
              which is to say
rushed glances
      and pretending
otherwise              or


              fluffed feather
followed by flight
      each fiber damp
                    and libidinous
each sunless crevice
      begging to be seen

men of skin
      and water
calloused fingers
              clinging, latching,
enraptured
      in the risk of being
                    swept away

# Lethargy

Brackish breath. Lifeline.
    Living elsewhere now.
        Daybreak they call it: lush

        and liquid sky, consultation
with the sun, walls
which angle like shadows.

Aubade, a house, a hot-
    breath whisper of wind—
        and you behind curtains of steam.
            Always a question. Small talk
              and wonderment. Wonder
         if the neighbors know by now.
      Bed, other bed, closed door.
   So many things to notice. So many
heavy eyes. And each time they open

        another day on fire. I could wake
    elsewhere if I tried. And wonder:
from whose vantage point

should I suffer today? Under
    whose sky? Always a question.
        Eyelids playing door hinge.

# Halving my Antidepressants with a Kitchen Knife

To wane like the moon
or to wean from,
wean off—

meaning which:
to be less or want less
from wanting?

Each spliced pill
a bleating sheep,
each surrounding crow

snow-capped
and on the cusp
of crisis. Tell me:

who determines
the sky's dose
of moon each night

and who is the man
just below the horizon
so eager to swallow it?

# B-Side to Depression

this morning I woke up happy
            found the day in a sunny-cool car
        topped with French roast and cream

discovered a heat inside my belly
            that was something more than stomach acid
        and it was that warmth

that moved my body from its cocoon
            of rigid routine and discount cereal
        a warmth so deep it lifted my body

like a premonition, a yellowjacket
            choosing an outfit from a wardrobe
        flipped for spring

for each year the winter sting
            gives the sun her voice back
        and each year it sounds more like an apiary

# Italian Water Garden

Lascivious, isn't it? The look of it
from the viewing deck like velvet
miniatures, lush with pastel pools
and singing fountains, the lindens
and ivy fresh from pruning. Under
the hush of falsetto fountains
there's a whispering. Statues calling
your name. Not the frog figure
whistling bridges of water but one
of the baskets overflowing with lime-
stone fruit. You take a piece from the basket
and bite into it, suddenly think your tooth
has chipped on the tough stone,
this crystalline shard in your mouth
leaving behind the bitter sting of dry wine.
And now, this bitten-into ball,
which was once apple or pear or plum,
fissures and fractures, opens like a geode—
in fact, it could very well be a geode
with its worlds-inside-world wonder:
tiny turquoise pools, jutting jade topiaries,
waves of rippling agate. And about now
you notice another sound, something
big band and brass, so you cup one
half of the fossilized fruit to your ear,
then the other. The music is clearer this way
but still far-away sounding, as if the ensemble
was enclosed inside another stone-
carved orb. And there's the whispering
again. Your name. A wisp of wind
with yet another clue to decipher.

# Vertical Garden

Nuzzle your cheek to the wall
like mother's sweater, let it engulf you

like a trick of warmth played
by the shadows of palm leaves.

If the scene needs action, bring in
love from the land, and more breath.

Here, the wall stands proud like a parade
but as quiet as when wind stops blowing.

And the door at center quieter still:
block metal like a guard at the gates

of grandiosity. Yet the surrounding branches
shift just slightly to shape out a living future.

There are infinite systems in the splitting sprigs,
timelines so easy to miss—as if

we walked through the door or past the door,
turning here, there, pausing to nuzzle close:

a brief moment while the door is still shut,
close enough for the plants to map your face.

## Summer in the Square

On sunny days, rainbows in the piss of the cherub.
We walk the fountain rim like a labyrinth, pick our pockets
in search of coins and conviction. For each penny flicked
there is a wish that never learned to swim. Nothing wished

comes true anyway. Wishes are merely prayers in need
of resuscitation. Or maybe it's the other way around:
prayers, wishes. We yearn for more but get washed away
in falsities and fluids. Even shame tastes chlorinated.

But if we wet our feet and walk the fountain fast enough,
we could trigger a vortex. Have you ever played wishing well
with an event horizon? It's simple. Sacrifice yourself
to the singularity, then swim free.

# II.

# Site Plan

[1]

Draw borders with air
and say mine, say money,

consider what it means to claim land—
how absurd to think one could own the earth.

Then linger on the thought of breaking ground.
What it means to break.

Promise yourself this is for something greater
than simply making a mark.

[2]

Gather stones and call it gold.
The cheap sound of oblong shapes
click-clacking in a pocket. At the bank,
pile the stones on a desk. A man
stands behind another man,
says, *Nice doing business.* Says, *Thank you.*

Say to the man, *This land is my land.*
Sing it aloud and think, *But not completely.*
Remind yourself of how you used to only dream
of death, but of how you can only now
dream of closing windows, as if
those ideas were entirely separate         things.

[3]

Carry wood.
Play graph paper
with ground.

Outline the footing
as if footing
wasn't something
you've tried to gain

since young man
became grown.

More borders
I suppose. Threshold
upon threshold.

[~]

There is an idea of a house before there is a house. Size,
shape, number of bedrooms. Ideas. Baths divvied up into
wholes and halves.

All of this is air: a blueprint of implication. Where does it
end? Property lines, of course, but look up. Look how high.

[~]

Ask yourself:

What makes a limit?

[4]

Pour the foundation. Or better yet,
draft a new origin story. No one
here beforehand. No such thing
as bones, as slaughter. History
is objective until it's talked about.
Houses are merely possibilities
until they're acted upon.

[5]

So act upon it. Construct your frame.
Take the corpselike wood
lying in pitiful piles
and whisper life back into their mouths.

Allow them to hold hands.
Let them kiss where their corners meet.

[~]

Ask yourself:

How many ballads can one write for right angles?

[6]

Apply sheathing. Hold ceremony.
All the things walls keep out.
All the things they keep inside.

Two ideas that will stand the test of time.
Inside. Outside. Inside. Outside.
Inside. Out.

[7]

Take a stubby pencil from your pocket,
find something to write on: paper towel,
an exposed beam. Draft equations

even God doesn't understand.

Remember: you're building a house.
Acknowledge the stress of it. This
on top of everything else there is

to worry about.

Try to leave. Find an exit. Or try
your hand at quantum physics. Walk
into the wall enough times

and see yourself through.

[8]

Mull over physics until your head hurts.

Add ice to your forehead. Bandage it up.

[~]

Ask yourself:

What would it take for the walls
                              to step aside?

What would it take for them
                              to push back?

[9]

Stop thinking. Punch a hole in the wall.
Invent window. Discover doorway.

[~]

            This opens up the prospect for passage,
      and there's a lot of opportunity here—for you
and wind and morningtime. Other things as well.

Light, luxury. Electric wires that weave
      through a labyrinth of connectivity,
            myriad throughways for which

            things come to pass. Pipes of all kinds.
      Tiny tunnels that snake up and down
and over. Ventilation. Plumbing.

The art of it all. The notion
      of movement and possibilities
            abound.

[10]

Stand in a room
or the space

that will soon
become a room.

It doesn't matter
which room you pick,

which space. Just stand
in it. Stand there

and look up
from the wood-

frame box.
No longer comes

the brooding
over limits

or if ownership
can extend its way

into stratosphere.
There are larger things

to consider.

[11]

Tell the sky it's complicated.
Tell the sky you need your distance.
Tell the sky what you need to tell it.
Tell the sky about the sun.
Tell the sky it gives joy but not always.
Tell the sky the sun has hurt you too.
Tell the sky no.

Tell the sky it doesn't have the right to victim blame.
Tell the sky it's complicated.
Tell the sky you are filing for divorce
Tell the sky in a language it understands.
Tell the sky with slanted beams.
Tell the sky with an overlay of shingles.
Tell the sky you're sorry and mean it.

[~]

Ask yourself:

If today's notion of property and land ownership are ideas rooted in harm[1], how can our homes remain symbols of success and shelter and safety without perpetuating the factors upon which they were founded?

[~]

Ask again:

What makes a limit?

                                                Ask yourself:

                                Where do we draw the line?

[12]

Use a mask when it comes time for the insulation.
Hide behind a veil of woven fibers and mouth
the questions you've been too afraid to ask.
If you're brave, write your questions down.
Seal them away behind the drywall and move on.

---

[1] Colonialism, overindulgence, greed, regard for self over community, excess, entropy, the perpetuation of pain in which we all play a part

[13]

Add light. Play God.
Lay flooring and then dance upon it.

Celebrate by taking more
from the earth:

        quartz, granite—

        chisel and carve and sand and—

[~]

Ask yourself:

What else? What more will men remove and displace?

[14]

Draw borders with air
and say, *This is it—*

*This is my home now.*

[~]

Ask yourself:

What now—now that this home is ready for occupants?

[~]

Answer:

Disregard the whirring sound,
the whispers from behind the walls,       the demons

                deep below the foundation—

[~]

Answer:

Lock the windows. Deadbolt the door.

[~]

Better to fear what's outside
than look too closely into a mirror.

III.

# On Learning my Grandfather Was Born in the U.S.

If I were to watch a Palermo cliff
corrode into the Tyrrhenian wake,
which 12th century cathedral
would ask me back to pray? Which
would scold me for misgendering the sea
an ocean or my grandfather
a native man? Which would steal my shoes
and speak in the forked tongue
of the family's late patriarch? Tongue
like memories taking the form
of swollen feet, toes amputated
and elsewhere. On Thanksgiving Day
we swam to shore with all ten toes
and prayed over a vulture we found
by a seaside cathedral. We said grace
by plucking leaves and hacking bark
from the family tree. We gave thanks
and forced splinters into our sternums,
unsure whether our bodies
would reject the shards like a new organ
or welcome them warmly like souvenir relics
bought abroad and blessed with seawater.

## Abduction GIF

consider: patterns
                of moon-skin
        and sky cattle
the wont
                and wanting
        one in the same
entire towns
                bound with corn
        silk and husk
trying their best
        to crop circle
                their way out
of inequity

## Harvest Poem

fire red when felled and once
    part of a larger body      womb-bound first
          then flower     and before long
flesh      never with the dream of being tooth-stabbed
     or cut open       stem
    not a stem but a hand-holding     a hand
holding an orb and the orb life itself
        life containing roots thick and strong
      to which it is then followed beyond the ground
    and there: a flower flowering fruit
      a blossom woven into myth and carmine
   for we once were seeds   patient
once part of a tree   timber-strong
      and look at us now     basket-ridden rot
   grainy throw-aways in a bushel of plastic mesh
   and bruising
could we have been flowers instead     real flowers I mean
   or maybe a grove of tremendous trees
  tremendous bodies / thriving bodies / bodies unfelled
   our offspring red and bald and blanched
   and afforded enough time to transform
       into paunch little doctors—
and one summer     maybe     one of the doctors
     visits the market
   paunch little doctor purchases a paunch little apple
       portrait of apple as ball gag
     mouth guard for spit-roast swine
and elsewhere / elsewhen
   an apple falls from a tremendous tree
  and yet      a stake finds its way through flesh
before it can learn the way of gravity     (what it is
     and what it isn't)
  before it could possibly know the doctor's hands
   the pig's teeth
but by the end it doesn't matter  by the end
  everything is red    everything
the whole world on fire
  the entire world in flames

# Months After the Chainsaw
# the Tree Speaks Back

Resist, it says, but means resuscitate.
Bugs feed on slime flux,
bubbling like pasta water, like sun-
burnt blisters. And what now?
Bleach? Vinegar?
When I later pour the gasoline,
I think of the boy from town,
the plot of land still for sale.
All this to say
there are certain things I miss about you.
I pick a mushroom and place it
to my ear like a telephone.
It speaks to me in translation,
in fragments from a famous elegy.
All this to say we are culpable.

# Human History as Deep Tissue Massage

Cradled. Face through a hole.
Relief between bursts of pointed pain.
And before you know it, time runs out.
Time goes on then runs out again.
Space folds in on itself.
The smell of lavender fields and burning.

# Long-Term Side Effects

How does anything begin?
What does it mean, before?

Life crawls from the ocean,
blood goes unchecked.

With so much misery
and medicine, I'm surprised

I never dreamed you
a war nurse.

Later, Lily jokes
about your tree-hair,

though she has yet to learn
about mycorrhizal networks,

the understory
of maternal endurance.

You see a specialist,
invest in ice helmets, curse

the medicine that once saved you.
Dad helped with the needles then,

a prescription that pinched too hot.
But resilience is the mouth

of a feral beast. It bites hard and locks.
I think, *Those jaws must get so tired,*

but remember then the workbench,
the vise, the handle you turned

with every last bit of strength.
Then comes the day

the doctor declares "cured."
Cured: such a kind word.

But kindness never lasts long
on this planet. Wartime lingers

like cold cloths growing warm
across your eyes.

Are celebrations ever sustainable?
Mother, is there always an aftermath?

# What is the Cube Root of Memory

The past  has us passed out in attic rooms

   six to a futon bed,

eyes heavy after sucking  smoke

   from lawn ornaments—

or younger   sun-kissed in a coastal cottage

   waiting for the clang

of brass handles  your uncle's ghost was said

   to pluck like harp strings.

Later in the log cabin  we discovered

   a minister's robe

and danced   until blasphemy became buoyant

   like belly laughs—

or later still in a moment yet to come

   in which we float

to a riverbed loft  lined with moon jellies and glassworks

   from our hometown.

What is it called  this thing between living

   and luster,

standing present  inside moments passed

   and others yet to come?

# Lullaby at Overtoun

*A mysterious and fatal history surrounds Overtoun Bridge in
West Dunbartonshire, Scotland, where dogs have been known
to jump off the bridge to the rocks 50 feet below.*

So says the bridge, This is where dogs leap
to their deaths. Every surrounding structure
tuned in, nodding with loose gravel,

for every platform, every overpass
is an altar from which to ponder—

the story of a shadow, the long-
drawn exhales of townsfolk and self.

At home, after being talked down,
there's the entire internet to browse
to take one's mind off such ruthless gravity.

There's a website to stream movies,
another to advise if a dog dies in any of them.

Collectively, the man's family chooses a documentary
on birds, and the birds dance, so silly

the way their bodies jerk in black-winged ballet,
in feathery folk dance: movements
made for mating. Such brilliant tweeting sounds,

a stunning orchestral score, but not a single birdsong
to remind the family of their fatal flaw,

that their wings, not-wings, are merely shoulder blades,
as limited in movement as the moon's rotation.

So says the bridge, says the shadow, says the self,
Even the wandering albatross cannot remain forever
afloat. For flight is as much a farce as forever is.

Even in dreams, a floating dog can hold as much weight
as a diving bell, descending deeper into dark waters.

# Vanishing Point

[1]

mapped by mathematics
        each moment is a still-life in intimacy
wood knots and crystal caves
                        golden hour, golden boy
a sun which follows the two of us
                on back roads, around a curve

        where geese graze in a cow pasture—
then, by way of steering wheel and dinner plans
                no, by way of metaphysics and husbandry
        we mimic motion and matrix
follow the road as far as the gardens—

how few animals there are now
                how little movement

[2]

wherein *everything* (whether word or vice)

cannot (scientifically, mathematically)

exist alongside (the concept of)

*nothing* (                                    )

[3]

and now
        our little life:

                how little life there is

# Nature Documentary

It starts with a thousand fiery collisions.
Even at its calmest
things are exploding.

Land forms from lava, lizard-like things
creep from the coast.
Language develops. Cities.

Conflict. Climate. To be continued…

The phenomenon of human evolution
and critical thinking.
And yet we're still at war.

Which is to say: failure, entropy.
In which all human endeavors
lead to more fire.

# Late Space

I'm waiting for space to approach time
the way sound races behind
some Mach-numbered aircraft,
fast and nervous like locker room glances.
Space is just doing its best existing.
Time on the other hand
acts exactly as one would expect time to act.

Theory: If one can be late in terms of time,
then one must be able to be late in terms of space.

A late space, if you will—solar significance in still dark,
nullity tucked in a trench on the Kelvin scale,
sun gods corroding like ancient papyrus.

Theory: If I could condense spacetime, if I could pull it
like a string, if I could just get it to bend...

I can ask the gods if that's what you want—
Helios post-hospice, Apollo palsied and pale,
some unnamed goddess
shriveled in her brightly colored nightgown.

Theory: You are far from where I wait.
You are at the beginning, the start of infinity.

And so I think back to when we were on the same plane,
the two-dimensional spacetime of us,
the ends of time swaying like polar-wind branches.
This was back when we thought
the golden spiral meant something,
back when we tried to keep up
with transcendental numbers.

Theory: In that dense and molting pinprick of energy,
the one where it all started, that's where
I'll find you again.

If I can ever find the courage to leave.
If I can ever preexist.

# Theory of Everything

Define poem.
Self-portrait as habitual knuckle-cracking.
Self-portrait as habit.
In other words, self-portrait as knuckles.
Always something cracking.
As with anything—poems, knuckles—
it starts and ends with air.

## Order of Operations

The bones inside my body have a PhD
in mechanical engineering. For weeks
after I broke my arm, the severed ulna
sprouted a baby bone bridge
that reached across waterways to connect
our peoples again. Later, when I punched a tree

and dislocated knuckle to some southern state,
the former ultimately found its way back home,
back north. That is not to say my body is a home.
Home is something else altogether:

a framework fixated on things stuck
inside of it. Bones as pet store goldfish. Bones
as boxes in the crawl space. And sometimes
my body can't sleep. Sometimes the sponge
that is my brain inside the skull that is my head
remembers that hands are skeletons all their own.

27 bones resting next to my pillow. A figure
I thought would have been a prime number
but isn't. And yet these metacarpals
could teach AP algebra if they had to.
Would ask you to solve for $x$
when $x$ is a boneyard of forearms.

And by adulthood, humans are left with 206 bones
though we are born into the world
with 64 more of them inside of us.
It's not that 64 bones just disappear. Bones
fuse together, become stronger. As in,

my depression was a bone and my anxiety
was a bone and now they are one ball of stress
inside a single swollen throat. And so finally,
the prime number I was searching for—
stronger now and ready to solve
for whatever equation you throw its way.

# A Familiar Glow

Who isn't fascinated by the sun?
A collapsed nebula
of molten gas large enough
to hold one million Earths
inside of it. And yet
from this point of view
on the blue planet, the sun
is the size of a coin
held up to the afternoon sky.
Of course, the sun is more
than an ornament,
more than a white-hot orb
of hydrogen and helium;
the sun is a gift-giver, a friend,
a cosmic letter
of love and light.
And while science
can explain
so much, some things
are left uncertain.
But here's what we know:
it takes eight minutes
and twenty seconds
for the sun's light
to reach Earth, meaning that
if the sun were to
mysteriously vanish one day,
it would take a full eight-
and-one-third minutes
for the people on Earth
to realize that anything
was wrong in that faraway
still-hot openness.
And then the sun
would be gone,
nil, nothing, and yet people
would have nowhere
to look but the sky for answers.
Confused eyes would study

the not-nighttime night
with bewilderment
and suspicion,
where a small but in-focus Jupiter
would remain illuminated
for an additional thirty minutes
until the light that reflected
from the distant giant
could reflect no more.
Then would come darkness,
dropping temperatures, panic.
Panic, panic, panic—
as if that's anything new.
And there are so many ways
this could go: a sizzling,
a slow and steady burning-out,
or the sun bloating
like an enflamed balloon,
placing the Earth
in its fiery mouth.
Or maybe you come up
with your own story.
Once upon a time, the sun
had enough of its life
in the Milky Way.
The sun says hello
to quantum tunneling
and goodbye to no one.
And so, as it goes,
the sun disappears.
Here's what we don't know:
How many would choose
to join if they could?
Who would tag along
and leap
to god-knows-where?
Sacrifice a body's mass
to another body's mass?
A matrimony, like fusion.

A covalent bond.
Hoping, always hoping,
not knowing exactly
how or when.
But there are always numbers,
mathematical constants.
Counting as well: one, two, three,
all the way to five hundred—
the time in seconds it takes
for the sun's light to reach Earth.
Now begin again, counting one, two,
over and over,
counting, waiting—
until the world turns dark
like a kitchen light switched off.
And there's an opening! A trapdoor!
And then: opened eyes,
a new world. A distant plane
with a familiar glow.
The heat of a hand-holding.
Do you ever consider the multiverse?
A theory that says everything
that can happen does happen.
Meaning that somewhere,
at some time, whether
in the past or future
or right this very instant,
you notice something strange,
of something incomprehensible.
Do you feel it,
this fearlessness?
Do you walk toward
the almost-kind-of-light
and extend your hand
in greeting? In a way,
that's exactly what this is.
A greeting, a pull,
a tenacious tugging—
but it gets stronger, denser,

and there's a sound,
or the opposite of sound,
something like a warmth
that can mean nothing other
than *Come along, welcome.*
There is an embrace,
the tickle of body hair.
And there you are,
leveling your gaze,
looking around,
wondering—

# Field Notes from the 21 Gram Experiment

*(Duncan MacDougall, 1866–1920)*

on the other side of the room, a light source
several pinpoints marching in place
there's a lamp on the table, other lamps in other places
a universal constant somewhere in the balance
six patients, a bedridden lamp, lights

                here and there

                    and elsewhere.

hovering.

incandescence
            floating,           lingering.

we make note of it: lamp on the table, lighting above
lives on top of beds on top of floor scales
body: a place light must taper out
floor scales counting in fractions
bodies doing things bodies have been known to do

                which is to say

                    light in the room

light

doing light things

closure cloaked somewhere in the gradient
so we count: bodies, physician, others in observation
and who are we who have lost count of the light
and why is it each time we blink light crawls

                into another

                    deeply dark space?

# Greetings from Somewhere in Spacetime

The greens are brighter somehow. The grass
not grass but a speaker for soundscapes,

yard songs like forcefields, pulsing
with peace and purpose, sermon-like,

the way cool air fills the lungs
with both rest and waking. Every day

is today if one considers physics. Or
think instead in terms of reflectance curves.

Yes, today is glowing green, hedge-like,
untrimmed because it's a wild hedge

without ties to property or pension, waving
in the wind like ceremony, like couplets

printed on glassine paper
then gently placed atop pool water,

which is to say, we are outside again:
the mating song of crickets

bowing wings with wings, an orchestral movement
under the guise of question, wondering

if today is actually today, as in
the moment one thinks of as now. Nevertheless,

time goes on with its many shades of green—
lime and pickle and pear—and so many sounds:

crickets and cicadas, the buzzing of bees,
but man-made things too: motors, machines

of all types. One could call it a symphony
if they were kind, but the world is never kind.

A cricket dies of old age after ten weeks.
The earth swallows everything.

A hideous, hungry caterpillar the earth is, until again
it is leafy and green, blissful in its budding.

Time passes and then it's the sun's turn to swallow.
More time and then there is something else.

A cosmic flower, dark with pull. A black hole
that never covers its mouth when it yawns.

# Diptych Self-Portrait

In two hours, at some point
in the past, I will be pulled
from an incision made
in my mother's abdomen.
Nurses will clean her up,
clean me up, do what they have to do.
Later, the six o'clock news
will show President Reagan
making his first major speech on AIDS.
That's the history lesson for the day,
an introduction to queer theory
and throes. Thirty-three years later
I sit in a room of my house
I never know how to name
and write this poem from that name-
less nook. I think of Jennifer Tonge's
birthday poem: she writes,
*My spring is gone.*
My spring, too, is gone—
that is, until a teal-tufted bird
breezes by the window and quivers
midair. I watch it flicker like a glitch
and I am lifted from the room
and from my mother and from the sky.
The day is blue again, like birthdays,
like bachelor's button flowers: every feather
and every wisp weightless in flight,
every wish and wonder—
And then I see the blue bird blink.
Both eyes, both wings,
and so, too, the wall clock.

# Self-Portrait as Search for Beauty

How can I compete with pearl oysters
or Picasso? Pollinators
perched on bearded irises

like drag queens perched at mirrors
bejeweled in goldenrod flecks
of gold and golden pollen?

Consider Chopin's nocturnes,
fifth-century ceramics,
self-portrait as self-pity

as if prayer was a plea
for caffeine and dormancy
to paradox their way
into philosophy and art.

What is the half-life
of a half-decent poem?
What good is one good harvest

after the honeycrisps
have rotted away,
when every shoe sole
is a magnet for soil?

Rumi said, *There
are hundreds of ways
to kneel and kiss the ground.*

And yet all we do to the ground
is walk senselessly over it.

# Guided Meditation

All of this is difficult to measure. Oxygen
on the intake, tickle of nose hairs. Then
the long-drawn draft of an exhale, poem
leaving the body, a burst of blackbirds
from the throat. You lie still, scan the body.
But nothing is ever truly still, is it? Stillness
in its truest form leads directly to decomposition.
There is no peace. There is never peace.
An entire skeleton, right now, inside of you.

# Poem with Locked Box

I have read the news differently ever since:
the names, the numbers. Nothing

exists now that isn't a reminder of trauma.
Even the term for this is trigger.

I pick up the phone. Such few times
I've heard my father's voice like this.

And the word he uses: shot. So mundane
until it's married to someone you love.

The flash I saw, the blinding white-
silver of shock, as if it presented a portal,

a wink from the multiverse, in which
everything is covered by the veil of what if.

The first recorded use of a gun
was in 1364, a leap year. Leap to

any future date and find a record
of sorrow in every second since.

Long before the gun, Ancient Greeks
theorized infinite worlds. Sometime later,

Schrödinger appears. From there,
we step back about a century—

there is no good news here except
that metaphysics doesn't speak

in amendments. Which is to say—
or rather, which is to theorize

an alternate reality. One in which
my brother isn't bleach splattered

under x-ray, one in which his friends
survive. A place in which I can freely pop

my bubblegum without transporting
my father-in-law back to the battlefield.

In this heaven, there is no word for bullet.
But who can possibly believe in heaven

when Schrödinger points his gun
at every locked box he sees?

And to think these are our success stories:
the invention of violence

our people's greatest innovation.

# Portrait of Us with Steam

Not every poem needs to be an elegy.
Let us write today about love: lilac love
that whispers down one's spine,
sudsy soft with sea salt and lavender.
Find vulnerability there,
for what is existence if not vigor?
Call it *Portrait of Us with Steam.*
Call it molecular movement.
Now breathe in—yes, just like that:
in, in. More. Can you feel it?
The euphoria of a fog-wet world
laced with tea tree and almond,
each note with the intention
of letting go, of diving in.
Each speck of condensation
cosplaying as a summer day
if not a softening of entire histories.
Each moment with water is revival,
reverence, a poetic retelling
of SS Poseidon as the ship
lifts from the sea. Watch
as it travels upward—
a weathered wedge mid-air
where thousands of aubades
are mistaken for raindrops,
collected into cedar buckets,
and later ladled
onto sizzling hot stones.

# Compost This Poem

and sign *Apple* in the place for witness.
In another space: *Shining Sun*.

Consider mushrooms and microbes,
all the ways we coexist with magic.

Because beyond every pane of glass
is a garden and beyond every garden

is a sky. Rain falls and continues to fall
but gently, feather-like.

Clouds share their gradients of salt
and clay. And far off in the distance,

the faint chime of bells carried
like a newborn by the tenacious wind.

# Notes

"Nine Panels" is an ekphrasis after "Things are Queer" by Duane Michals.

"In Which the Sauna Becomes a Sacrament" is for Joetta.

"Halving my Antidepressants with a Kitchen Knife" references elements in August Friedrich Schenck's painting "Anguish."

"Italian Water Garden" was inspired by an area of the same name at Longwood Gardens in Kennett Square, PA.

"On Learning My Grandfather Was Born in the US" was reprinted in issue 21 of *Dark Mountain*.

"What is the Cube Root of Memory" is for Matt.

"Summer in the Square" borrows a line from Louise Glück.

"Poem with Locked Box" borrows a line from luna rey hall.

# Acknowledgments

Thank you to the editors of the following publications in which the following poems, sometime in different form, first appeared:

*Alien Magazine:*  "Lullaby at Overtoun"

*Bending Genres:*  "What is the Cube Root of Memory"

*Every Pigeon:*  "B-Side to Depression"

*Maudlin House:*  "Late Space"

*No Contact:*  "A Familiar Glow,"
"Self-Portrait as Search for Beauty"

*Okay Donkey:*  "Greetings from Somewhere in Spacetime"

*Palette Poetry:*  "Poem with Locked Box"

*Soft Punk:*  "Compost This Poem,"
"Condensation,"
"Diptych Self-Portrait"
"Field Notes from the 21 Gram Experiment,"
"Portrait of Us with Steam,"
"Renewal"

*RHINO:*  "Fever Dream as Cardio"

*Rogue Agent:*  "Order of Operations"

*Third Coast:*  "Harvest Poem"

*saltfront:*  "On Learning My Grandfather Was Born in the US" *the lickity~split:*      "Theory of Everything"

*The Lumiere Review*:      "Every Living Day"

*The Shore:*      "Italian Water Garden"

*The Shoutflower:*      "Abduction GIF"

*Yes Poetry:*      "Months After the Chainsaw the Tree Speaks Back"

# About the Author

Adam Gianforcaro is the author of the poetry collection *Morning Time in the Household, Looking Out*, and the children's picture book, *Uma the Umbrella*. His work can be found in *Poet Lore*, *Palette Poetry*, *Northwest Review*, *RHINO*, *Third Coast*, *Maudlin House*, *The Cincinnati Review*, and elsewhere.
He lives in Delaware.

# About the Publisher

Thirty West Publishing House

Handmade chapbooks (and more) since 2015

www.thirtywestph.com / thirtywestph@gmail.com

You should follow us! Consider being a patron?

Review our books on Amazon & Goodreads

@thirtywestph

www.ingramcontent.com/pod-product-compliance
Lightning Source LLC
Chambersburg PA
CBHW031548310726
48971CB00008B/2679